STERLING CHILDREN'S BOOKS

New York

An Imprint of Sterling Publishing
387 Park Avenue South
New York, NY 10016

ISBN 978-1-4027-7377-8 (HC)

Library of Congress Cataloging-in-Publication Data
Mayer, Mercer, 1943-
 [Little Critter's bedtime storybook]
 Little Critter bedtime storybook / by Mercer Mayer.
    p. cm.
 Previously published: Little Critter's bedtime storybook. New York : Golden Books, 1987.
 Summary: Finding Little Sister acting selfish, fussy, and grumpy and refusing to go
to sleep, Little Critter tells her three bedtime stories in which the characters reflect her bad
behavior.
 ISBN 978-1-4027-7377-8
 [1. Brothers and sisters--Fiction. 2. Behavior--Fiction. 3. Bedtime--Fiction.] I. Title.
 PZ7.M462Lai 2011
 [E]--dc22

                                                              2010039026

Distributed in Canada by Sterling Publishing
c/o Canadian Manda Group, 165 Dufferin Street
Toronto, Ontario, Canada M6K 3H6
Distributed in the United Kingdom by GMC Distribution Services
Castle Place, 166 High Street, Lewes, East Sussex, England BN7 1XU
Distributed in Australia by Capricorn Link (Australia) Pty. Ltd.
P.O. Box 704, Windsor, NSW 2756, Australia

For information about custom editions, special sales, and premium and corporate purchases,
please contact Sterling Special Sales at 800-805-5489 or specialsales@sterlingpublishing.com.

A Big Tuna New Media LLC/ J.R. Sansevere Book

Manufactured in China

Designed by 3&Co.

Lot #:
2 4 6 8 10 9 7 5 3 1
04/12

www.sterlingpublishing.com/kids

LITTLE CRITTER'S BEDTIME STORYBOOK

MERCER MAYER

STERLING CHILDREN'S BOOKS

New York

CONTENTS

Bedtime

"It's getting late," said Mom. "Time for bed."

"I should get to go to bed later," said Little Critter, "because I'm older."

"I don't want to go upstairs alone!" Little Sister complained.

"She keeps me awake," said Little Critter.

"I do not! I go right to sleep," said Little Sister.

Dad settled the argument. "You're both going to bed, so go on."
Little Critter and Little Sister marched upstairs, brushed their teeth, and got into bed.

"Good night, sleep tight," said Mom and Dad.

They turned out the lights. But Little Sister was not one bit tired . . .

The Fussy Princess

"I can't sleep without my bear," complained Little Sister. "I left it downstairs."

Little Critter yawned. "So go and get it."

"I'm scared to go downstairs alone."

Little Critter sighed and went to get Little Sister's bear. He got back into bed.

"This is my brown bear," Little Sister frowned. "I sleep with the pink one."

"Okay, okay," said Little Critter. "If I get the *pink* one, will you go to sleep?"

"Yes."

This time Little Critter brought the pink bear. He got into bed one more time.

"I think my fuzzy blanket is downstairs, too," said Little Sister.

"Why didn't you tell me that before?"

"I didn't think of it," said Little Sister.

"You don't need all that stuff in your bed to sleep," Little Critter said. "You are too fussy."

"What does 'fussy' mean?" asked Little Sister.

"I'll tell you a story about a fussy princess, and then you'll know," answered Little Critter.

"**Once upon a time**, a long, long time ago, there was a fussy princess who couldn't sleep unless everything was just right. She had to have her favorite blanket and all her dolls on her bed."

"You're telling a story about me. I don't like stories about me," said Little Sister.

"Are you a princess who lived a long, long time ago?" asked Little Critter.

"Well, no," admitted Little Sister.

"Then this story is not about you." Little Critter went on.

"The princess had to have everything just so at night. And she was no picnic during the day, either. All her dresses had to be perfectly pressed. If they had even the slightest wrinkle, she threw a fit.

"One day, a big dragon who lived in the mountains flew down to the castle. He had heard about the fussy princess and how her servants took care of her. It sounded like a good deal to him, and he liked the castle when he saw it. So he decided to move in. The first thing he did was throw out the king and his family.

"The royal family spent the night in the barn. The princess had to sleep with cows, donkeys, sheep, and chickens. Needless to say, she didn't sleep a wink.

"When the farmer found the family the next morning, he threw them out for trespassing. That night they had to sleep under a tree."

"I bet it rained," Little Sister chimed in.

"That's right." Little Critter nodded. "It rained, and they got all wet. The princess didn't slep that night either.

"By the third night, the princess was a mess. Her gown was torn and dirty. And was it ever wrinkled! Not only had her family been thrown out of the castle, but the dragon had her favorite blanket and her dolls. This was just too much. The princess threw a fit. She screamed until her father promised to go and get her things from the dragon."

"When I scream, Daddy makes *me* go sit in our room," said Little Sister.

Little Critter continued. "Her father went to the castle, pounded on the door, and told the dragon to open up. And that's just what the dragon did. He opened the door and blew his fiery breath at the king. The king ran back to his family under the tree, defeated and slightly scorched.

"So the princess made up her mind to do something herself. She would sneak into the castle that night when everyone was asleep.

"It was very late when she reached the castle. She crept upstairs to her room and found the dragon sleeping in her bed with her favorite blanket and all her dolls. Boy, was she mad."

"Wasn't she scared?" Little Sister wondered.

"Of course," Little Critter said. "But she was even more angry than scared."

"The princess was *so* angry that she went to the laundry room and got a bucket of soapy water. She threw it right in the sleeping dragon's face. The dragon woke up with a snort and a sputter.

"'Now you're gonna get it,' the dragon said to the princess.

"He glared at the princess and showed her his fangs. Now the princess was more scared than angry," said Little Critter. "She backed away toward the door. The dragon took a deep breath to blow fire at her—but all that came out were soapy bubbles! The princess had put out his fire."

"What did the dragon do?" asked Little Sister.

"He cried," said Little Critter. "No one had ever put out his fire before, and without it he couldn't be ferocious. He cried and cried.

"The king and the queen were worried sick when they discovered that the princess was missing. They figured she had gone to the castle, so they ran there as fast as they could. You can imagine their surprise when they burst in and found their daughter comforting a crying dragon."

"Were they mean to the dragon?" asked Little Sister.

"No. After he apologized for being so awful, they invited him to stay on as a guest."

"Anyway," said Little Critter, "the princess was so happy to be back in the castle that she decided not to be fussy anymore. She realized it didn't matter if her favorite blanket wasn't in just the right spot, or if one of her dolls was in another room."

"Is that all?" asked Little Sister.

"That's it. Now go to bed."

"But I can't sleep without my fuzzy blanket."

"Didn't you understand the story?" Little Critter asked.

"Yes, I did," replied Little Sister, "but I'm not a princess and there is no dragon in *my* bed."

Little Critter groaned. "If I get your fuzzy blanket, do you promise to go to sleep?"

"Yes, if you also get me a drink of water on the way back."

The Bear Who Wouldn't Share

Little Sister was still not asleep.

"What are you doing?" Little Critter asked.

"Nothing," said Little Sister. *Munch*, *munch*.

"You're eating something. Give me a cookie," said Little Critter.

"No!"

"Did you ever hear the story of the bear who wouldn't share?"

"No!"

"Then I'm going to tell it to you," Little Critter said.

"**Once upon a time**, Mr. Bear made pies and jams and all sorts of good things to eat and stored them in the back of his cave. You see, bears sleep all winter, and he wanted to make sure there would be a nice breakfast waiting for him when he woke up in the spring.

"He ate dinner, put on his soft pajamas, and crawled into bed, ready for a long winter's rest. But he hadn't dozed off for more than a month when he was awakened by a loud knocking at his door. There, huddled on his doorstep, was a little critter.

"The little critter said, 'Please Mr. Bear, would you let me come in? It has been the coldest winter ever, and I'm half frozen and half starved.'

"The bear thought it over. 'You can come in if you'd like," he said, 'but I'm just a poor bear and I have nothing to eat.'"

"That's not true!" Little Sister cried. "He has all those pies and other stuff he was saving!"

"I know," said Little Critter. "Just listen. The bear let the little critter sleep on the rug by the fireplace. Then he crawled back into his own bed. But soon he was awakened by another banging on the door. Now there was a family of cold, hungry rabbits on his doorstep.

"'I will let you in to warm yourselves,' said the bear, 'but I can't spare anything to eat.' So the rabbits snuggled down into a washtub. Then the bear went back to sleep."

"I don't like that bear," said Little Sister, reaching for another cookie.

"He was pretty selfish," agreed Little Critter. "Before long there was still more banging on the door. This time there were all sorts of forest animals on the doorstep. 'Come in,' Mr. Bear told them, 'but there's no food.'"

"The cave was crowded by this time, but everyone found a place to sleep. Then the bear nestled back into his bed. As he dropped off to sleep, he could hear the animals crying because they were hungry.

"That night, the bear had a dream. He dreamed that his conscience came to visit him."

"What's a conscience?" asked Little Sister.

"The part of you that tells you to be fair and to do good things," explained Little Critter.

"Oh," said Little Sister.

"The conscience asked the bear how he could just lie there like a big lump of fur and let the other animals starve. The bear tried to stick up for himself. He said, 'If I feed them all, I won't have anything left to eat in spring. Then *I'll* be hungry.'

"'Sweet dreams to you, then,' grumbled the conscience—and disappeared.

"But his dreams weren't *sweet*," said Little Critter. "They were about all those hungry animals.

"Suddenly, the bear jumped out of bed. 'I just remembered,' he said, 'I have a whole storeroom full of good things to eat.' He threw open the storeroom door and told everyone to dig in. Then he went back to bed and slept soundly.

"Finally spring came, and the bear woke up. He rubbed his eyes and looked around. No one was there. They had all gone back to their homes. He looked in the storeroom, but all that was left was one wrinkled apple. The bear was terribly hungry, and he was wondering what he was going to do when he noticed a pile of letters that had been stuck under his door. He opened one and read it.

"It said:

"Dear Mr. Bear:
Thank you for sharing your delicious food this winter. When you wake up in the spring, you must come to my house for breakfast.

Sincerely, the little critter who stayed in your cave"

"The bear opened more letters," said Little Critter, "and each letter was more wonderful than the last. Someone even promised to bring a feast right to his cave. A big tear came to Mr. Bear's eye, and he thought, 'Why, I have everything I could ever want this spring—food *and* friends.'"

"Here," said Little Sister, passing him the box of cookies.

"Hey! There's only one cookie left!" said Little Critter.

"That's because you told such a long story," Little Sister answered.

The Day the Wind Stopped Blowing

Little Sister was wide awake. She turned on the lights.

"The wind is blowing so hard that it's scaring me," said Little Sister.

Little Critter thought for a moment. "Did you ever hear the story of the day the wind stopped blowing?"

"No," said Little Sister. "Will you tell it to me?"

"Sure," said Little Critter, and he began.

"**Once upon a time**, the wind blew even harder than he does now."

"Why did he blow so hard?" asked Little Sister.

"It made him feel good," said Little Critter. "He blew so hard that birds had trouble flying and people had trouble walking. Sometimes he even blew the roofs off the houses.

"People got tired of the wind blowing so hard. They complained to the king," said Little Critter. "The king tried to stop the wind. He had a high wall built around the kingdom, but the wind blew it down. He sent the royal army out to stop the wind, but the wind blew them back.

"Then the king had signs tacked up, offering a huge reward to anyone who could get the wind to stop blowing. But the wind blew the signs down before anyone could see them."

"It sounds like he was mean," said Little Sister.

"No, he wasn't," said Little Critter. "I told you, blowing hard made him feel good. He didn't know he was causing trouble.

"Anyway, one of the signs blew right into the house of a little mouse and landed in his soup. The mouse read it and thought, 'I'll go to the palace and tell the king that I will get the wind to stop blowing.'"

"Did he know how to do that?" asked Little Sister.

"He wasn't sure," said Little Critter. "But he was tired of having things blow into his soup, and he hoped to win the reward. He was a poor mouse."

"Oh," said Little Sister.

"When the mouse told the king his plans, the king laughed. He didn't believe a little mouse could succeed where the king had failed. He threw the mouse out of the castle.

"Well, now the mouse was mad. He set out that very day to find the wind and get him to stop blowing. He walked for miles. The wind was blowing harder and harder, and it wasn't easy for the mouse to stay on his feet, so he knew he was going the right way. Finally, he got to the wind's house and knocked on the door.

"The wind invited the little mouse in. Right away, the mouse began yelling at him. He told him not to blow anymore, because no one appreciated being knocked around. He said he was acting like a bully and a meanie."

"What did the wind do?"

"Well, the wind was very surprised to hear all this, and his feelings were hurt. Without saying a word, he went upstairs and closed the door.

"After the wind left, the mouse noticed that the air was very still. Not even a tiny breeze was blowing. 'Hooray! I did it—I got the wind to stop!' he thought.

"The mouse started back to the castle. Along the way he noticed how hot it was now that there was no wind. And because there was nothing to blow clouds away, it had started to rain. Nobody looked happy.

"When the mouse marched into the throne room and demanded his reward, the king glared at him. He wasn't convinced that the mouse had been the one who made the wind stop, and, besides, he thought things were even worse than before. He threatened to put the mouse in the dungeon.

"The mouse ran out of the castle as fast as he could, all the way back to the wind's house. He knocked, but the wind wouldn't come to the door. 'Go away,' called the wind. 'Nobody likes me.'

"The mouse begged the wind to come out so they could talk. He apologized for being so rude before and told the wind how important he was to everyone.

"The wind cheered up a little. He agreed to start blowing again so long as every once in a while he was allowed to blow as hard as he liked. The mouse helped the wind to practice blowing until he knew what was just right and what was too hard.

"The mouse went back to the king and demanded his reward again. The king just laughed. Suddenly, the sky grew dark and a big storm blew right into the castle.

"'ARE YOU LAUGHING AT MY LITTLE FRIEND?' bellowed the wind.

"'Errr, why, no,' muttered the king. 'I was laughing because I am so happy to give him a big reward.'

"'BE SURE THAT YOU DO,' boomed the wind, who winked at his friend and then blew himself home.

"The king, true to his word, gave the little mouse the reward and made him the official royal weathermouse. The mouse was very happy,

thanks to the wind. So you see, the wind is friendly, and not scary at all."

"Is that the end of the story?" asked Little Sister.

"Yes, now go to sleep," said Little Critter.

"The wind is still a little scary, but your story has made me so sleepy, I think I'll go to sleep anyway."

Little Sister turned off the light and snuggled under the covers.

"Good. And good night," answered Little Critter.

Within minutes, Little Sister was sound asleep.

THE END